HiT entertainment

First published in Great Britain 2009 by Dean
an imprint of Egmont UK Limited
239 Kensington High Street,
London W8 6SA

© 2009 Prism Art & Design Limited, a HIT Entertainment company.
The Fireman Sam name and character are trademarks of
Prism Art & Design Limited, a HIT Entertainment company.
Based on an original idea by D Gingell, D Jones and
characters created by RMJ Lee

The Beast of
Pontypandy

One evening, Dilys Price was watching a television programme about wild cats.

Fireman Sam held a meeting about the beast in Bella's café.

"My Norman saw it first," said Dilys. "Oh, he was so brave."

"Mmm," said Sam. "This beast is probably just someone's idea of a joke. But I still want everyone to take care."

"We're worried about Woolly," said Sarah. "We haven't seen him today. You don't think the beast got him, do you?"

"I'm sure he's safe," said Sam. "Let's keep a lookout for him."

"I give-a big-a reward to anyone who help-a catch-a this-a beast," said Bella.

Norman smiled. "A reward," he said quietly. **"Great!"**

Norman, James and Mandy decided to look for the beast on Pontypandy Mountain.

"I'll stay here in town," said Sarah.

"We have our **walkie-talkies** to keep in touch."

Norman met James and Mandy
on their way to the mountain.
He hid Woolly behind a wall.

"Hi, Norman," said Mandy.
"We're going to find the beast.
Want to come?"

"Yeah, cool," said Norman with
a sly smile on his face.

Mandy, James and Norman
climbed up the steep
mountain path.

They didn't notice that Woolly was
following them!

It soon started to get dark.

Suddenly, Mandy heard something
behind them.

"What was that noise?"
she said.

"It's the beast," said Norman.
"It must be following us!"

"Run!" said Mandy.

Mandy and James ran off as quickly
as they could, leaving Norman
chuckling to himself.

Mandy and James ran along
the mountain path, but it soon
came to a dead end.

There was a steep drop where the
rest of the path should have been,
and they couldn't go
any further!

"Oh, no, we're stuck!
Call Sarah on her walkie-talkie,
James!" said Mandy. "Tell her
to send Fireman Sam!"

Back in Pontypandy, Sarah rushed to tell Dilys what had happened.

"Mandy, Norman and James are trapped on Pontypandy Mountain," she said. "Now the beast is after them!"

"Oooh!" said Dilys. "The beast has got my Norman! I'll never see his little freckled face again."

"You will," said Sarah. "I'll tell Uncle Sam. He'll save him."

Minutes later, the Fire Station alarm bell rang.

"Action Stations, everybody. We have an emergency," said Fireman Sam. "The children are stuck on the mountain and the beast has been spotted nearby!"

Sam, Elvis and Penny put on their helmets and jumped aboard Jupiter. The blue lights flashed, the siren wailed – **Nee Nah! Nee Nah!** – and they raced off.

Tom flew
the mountain
rescue helicopter
to Pontypandy Mountain.

He lowered the winch and lifted
Sam into the air.

"Over here!" yelled Mandy.

Tom lowered Sam down
to the path.

"Are you okay?" asked Sam.

"We're fine. But the beast is
over there," said James.
"In that bush."

Fireman Sam was carrying
a net to catch the beast.

Sam and Penny threw the net over the bush. They walked slowly towards it and found – Norman and the beast!

"I … er … saved James and Mandy," said Norman. "Look, I caught the beast too."

"Baaaa!" said Woolly.

Sam and Penny looked at each other.

"Woolly?" said Sam.

Later, Bella gave Norman his reward. It was a **huge cake!**

"What I don't understand is how Woolly got covered in all that mud," said Penny.

"And why was Norman all muddy when I saw him this morning?" said Sarah.

"Have you got something to tell me, Norman Price?" Dilys asked.

"Errr ... I made Woolly into the beast as a joke!" he said. "Sorry, Mam."

Dilys knew just how to teach
Norman a lesson.

"All right," groaned Norman.
"Jump into the sink, Woolly,
it's time for your bath."

"Baaaaa!" said Woolly.